Hello, My Name Is Octicorn

For Frankie and Milo
—K.D.

Book design by Dani Guralnick

Printed in the U.S. and funded with Kickstarter

ISBN-10: 0615873936
ISBN-13: 978-0-615-87393-0

Hi everyone. I'm Octi.

What?

Haven't you ever seen an octicorn before?

We're half octopus, half unicorn,
so okay, maybe we are kind of rare.

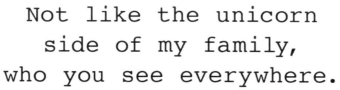

Not like the unicorn
side of my family,
who you see everywhere.

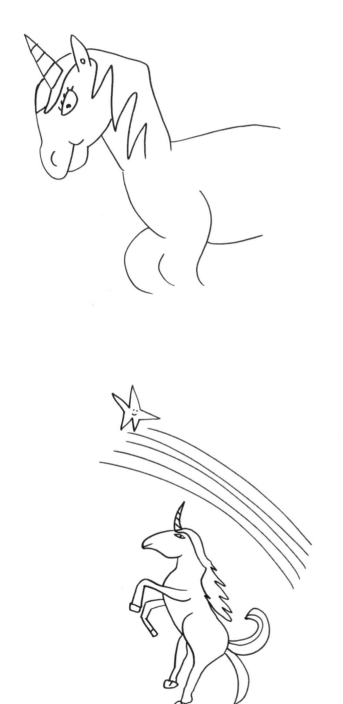

Personally, I don't get why
people like unicorns so much.
I mean even just the name. Unicorn.
Shouldn't it be uni-horn?

Where does the corn come in?

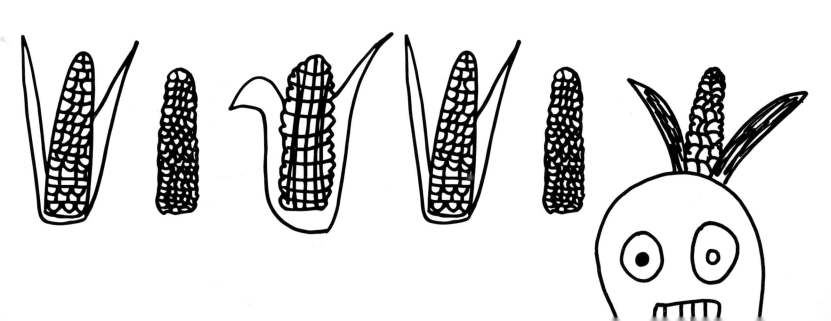

Plus if you ask me, unicorns
are a little full of themselves.

But back to me.

People always ask how I came to be an octicorn and how my parents met.

I think it was a costume party.

Or maybe a personal ad.

UNICORN
SEEKS OCTOPUS
FOR FUN, FRIENDSHIP, AND POSSIBLE STRANGE LOOKING OFFSPRING.

As far as I know, I'm the only octicorn there is.
Which sometimes makes it hard to fit in...

On land...

Or at sea...

And when you don't fit in,
you don't get invited to a lot of parties.

Which is too bad because octicorns are lots of fun at parties. For one thing, we can juggle like nobody's business.

For another,
we're quite good
at certain games,
like ring toss.

And if it happens to be a pool party,
octicorns are great at water sports.
(Even if there is the occasional
beach ball incident.)

So if you're having a pool party,
you should definitely think about
inviting an octicorn.

And if you're not having a pool party,
here's why you should definitely think about
having an octicorn for a friend:

Octicorns are good at lots of sports.

We're also terrific dancers.

Octicorns are excellent swimmers but...

What I really want is a jet ski.

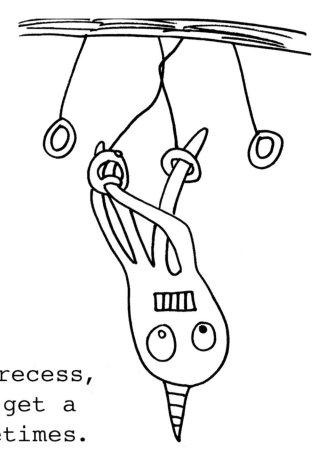

Octicorns love recess,
even if it can get a
bit tricky sometimes.

And we're also quite good at making s'mores.

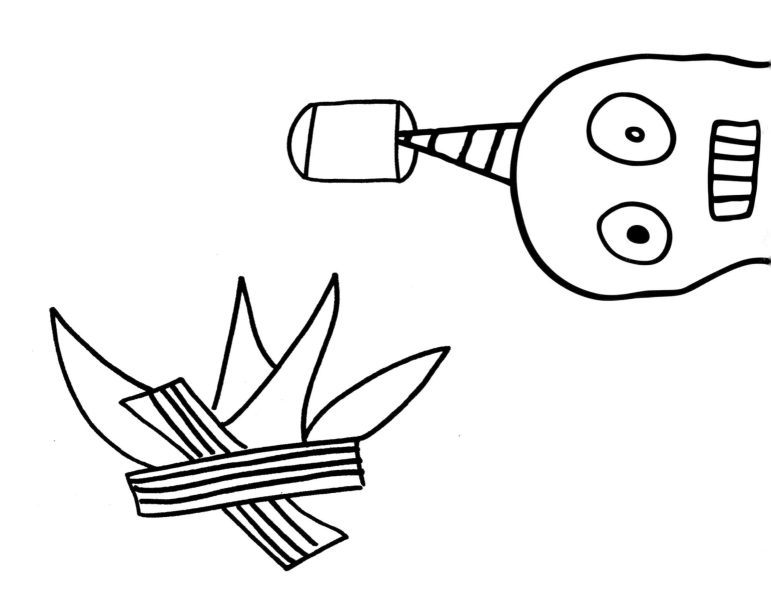

Octicorns love Christmas.

And our favorite color is blue, like the ocean or the sky or the way we feel at school sometimes.

(I know that's a feeling,
not a color, but still, octicorns like blue.)

Octicorns are extra good at hugging.

Octicorn hug anyone?

And if you're wondering what to serve an
octicorn for lunch, we love plankton, fresh clover...

...and also cupcakes.

Because who doesn't like cupcakes?

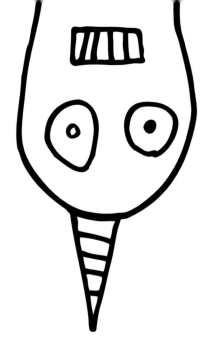

I know I look different than
everyone else, but that's ok.

Because in the end, we all want the same things:
cupcakes, friends and a jet ski.

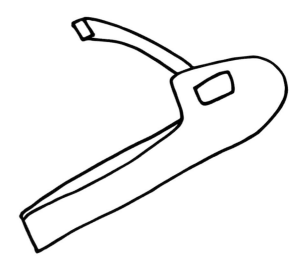

So, um...

Await your reply...

Love,
Octi

Supporters of Octicorn

Janet Champ

Rick McQuiston

Bill Davenport

The Von Selis Family

Dan Wieden

Elisa Silva

Jeffrey Hansen

Mikaylee O'Connor

Anna Rieke

Carly White

Damion Triplett

Mak, Ryder & Sam Johnson

Melanie Myers

Natalie P. Montgomery

Amie Diller

Shauna Diller

Ademar Matinian

Marciano Agabon

Kristi Hamlet

Denise Huie

Gretchen Treser

Matt Holmes

The Great Society

Jason Dahl

Beth Garrison

Kirk Iverson

Lizzie Schwartz

David M. Ortmann